Library of Congress Cataloging in Publication Data:
Roberts, Sarah. Don't cry, Big Bird. (Sesame Street start-to-read books) SUMMARY: Big Bird gets dis-
couraged because he is so much bigger than his Sesame Street friends. [1. Size and shape—Fiction]
I. Leigh, Tom.   II. Title.   III. Series.   IV. Children's Television Workshop.   PZ7.R54428Do
[E]   AACR2 81-4075   ISBN: 0-394-84868-3 (trade); 0-394-94868-8 (lib. bdg.)
Manufactured in the United States of America
15 16 17 18 19 20

A Sesame Street Start-to-Read Book™

Don't Cry, Big Bird

by Sarah Roberts · illustrated by Tom Leigh

**Featuring Jim Henson's
Sesame Street Muppets**

Random House/Children's Television Workshop

Big Bird liked to play
with his friends.
But playing with them
was hard for Big Bird
because . . .

their jump ropes were too short . . .

their hopscotch boxes were too small . . .

their hide-and-seek hiding
places were too little . . .

their see-saws came down
but never went up.

One day Big Bird came home
from the park by himself.
"I am too big to play
with my friends," he sobbed.

He was so busy crying
he did not see
his friend, Snuffle-upagus.

"Don't cry, Bird,"
said Snuffle-upagus.
"You are not too big.
Their games are too little."

Big Bird jumped up.
He stopped crying.
"Do you really think so,
Mr. Snuffle-upagus?"

"Yes, Bird, I really do,"
said Snuffle-upagus.
"You are a very nice size—
big, like me."

Then Big Bird had an idea.
"Hey, we are both big.
So let's play together!"
said Big Bird.

Snuffle-upagus shook his head.
"No, Bird, I can't play now.
It is time for my nap."
And Snuffle-upagus went slowly
down the street.

"It is nice to be big,"
Big Bird said sadly.
"But sometimes I wish I could
make myself smaller."

Back at the park Ernie and Bert
were thinking.
"If only Big Bird were smaller.
Then he could play with us,"
said Ernie.

"Well, we can't make Big Bird
smaller," said Bert.
"But maybe we can make
our games bigger ... like this!"
And he tied two jump ropes
together.

Grover ran to get Big Bird.
"We have a big surprise
for you!" said Grover.

When Big Bird got to the park,
Ernie and Bert were turning
the big rope.
"Jump, Big Bird!" they said.
Big Bird jumped.
The rope went over his head.
"Hurray for Big Bird!" they said.

Everybody had a turn
at jumping rope.
Then Betty Lou drew the
biggest hopscotch boxes ever.
"Come on, Big Bird, hop!"
she said.

Big Bird hopped.

Then he looked down.

"I did it right!" he said.

"I did not step on the lines!

Hurray for me!"

Big Bird was really happy.
Until he remembered something.
"I am still too big for
hide-and-seek," he said.

Then suddenly he smiled.
"Hey, everybody!" he shouted.
"I do not have to hide.
I can be IT.
I can look for YOU!"

Everybody played hide-and-seek,
and Big Bird was IT.

Then they played on the see-saw.

Big Bird sat on one end.

All his friends sat on the other.

The see-saw went up and down.

"What can we do now?"
asked Herry.
"Let's fly my new kite,"
said Betty Lou.

She held the string
and ran and ran and ran.
The kite began to fly.
It flew higher and higher.

Until it hit the top of a tree.
Bump! The kite fell down
and stuck in the tree.

"Oh no!" cried Betty Lou.

"I'll never get my kite back now."

Big Bird ran to Betty Lou.

"Don't cry," he said.

"I think I can help."

Big Bird stood on his tiptoes.
He reached high up
and pulled down the kite.

"Here, Betty Lou," said Big Bird.
"Your kite is as good as new."

"Hurray for Big Bird!"
everyone cheered.
Big Bird was very happy.

"Now let's play my favorite
game," he said.
"What game is that?"
everyone asked.
Big Bird smiled.
"Giant steps!"